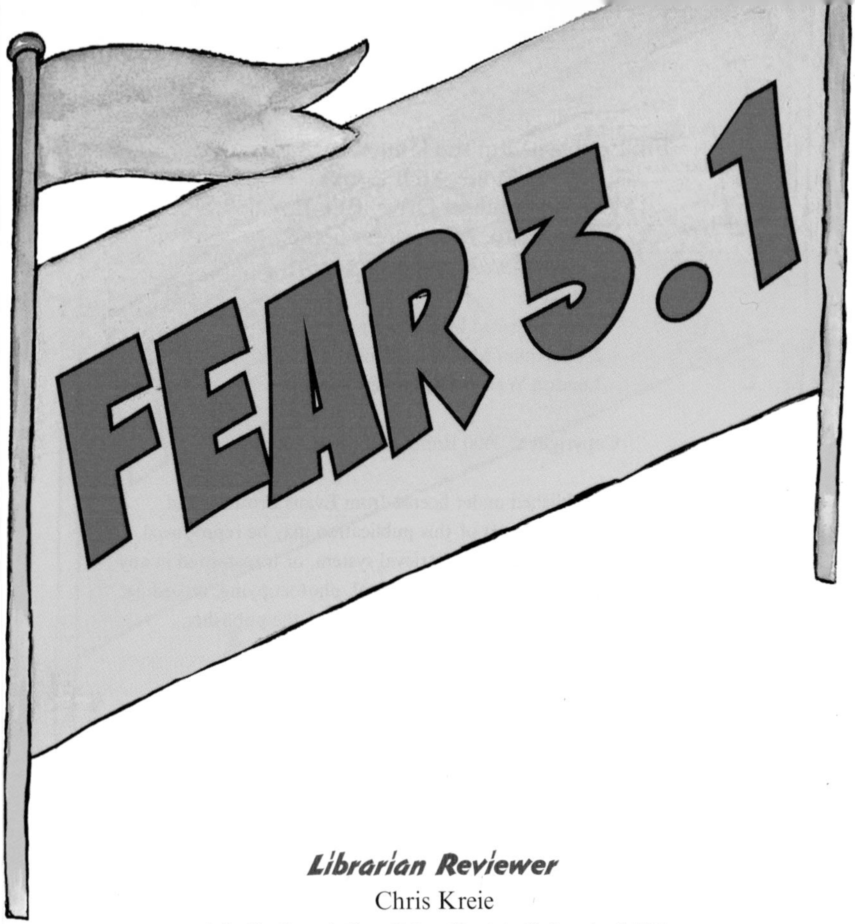
FEAR 3.1

Librarian Reviewer
Chris Kreie
Media Specialist, Eden Prairie Schools, MN
MS in Information Media, St. Cloud State University, MN

Reading Consultant
Elizabeth Stedem
Educator/Consultant, Colorado Springs, CO
MA in Elementary Education, University of Denver, CO

I belonged to the local scout troop. We did lots of camping and wilderness skills and that kind of thing, but my favorite activity was rock climbing on:

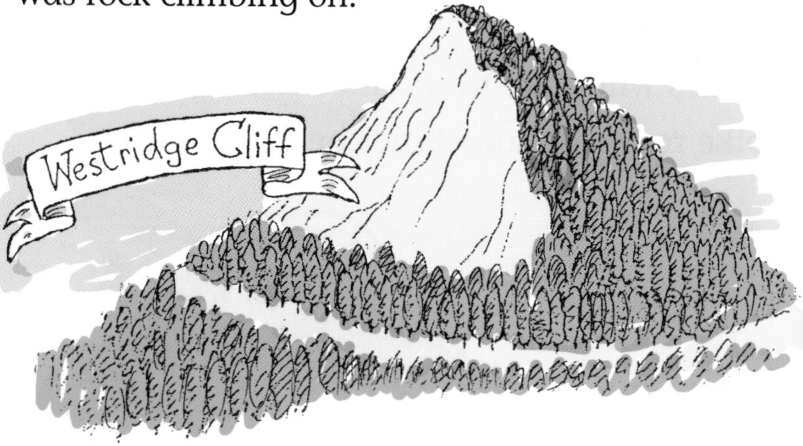
Westridge Cliff

We always had plenty of supervisors and training, and we always checked equipment carefully.

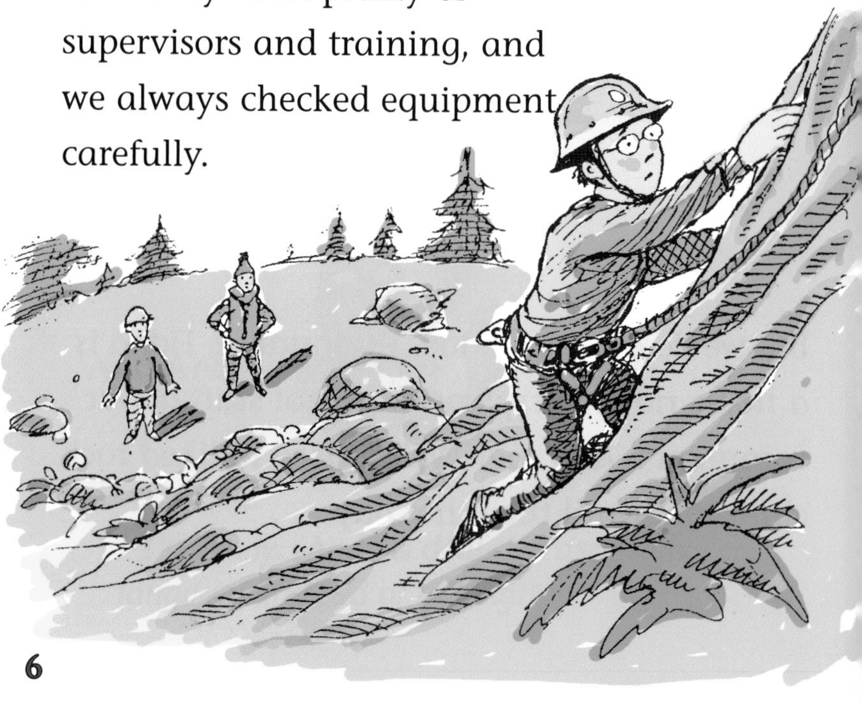

But sometimes there were problems. It was a part of the cliff I had climbed many times before. I was 100 yards up. I had just placed my foot in a crevice and was reaching for a handhold.

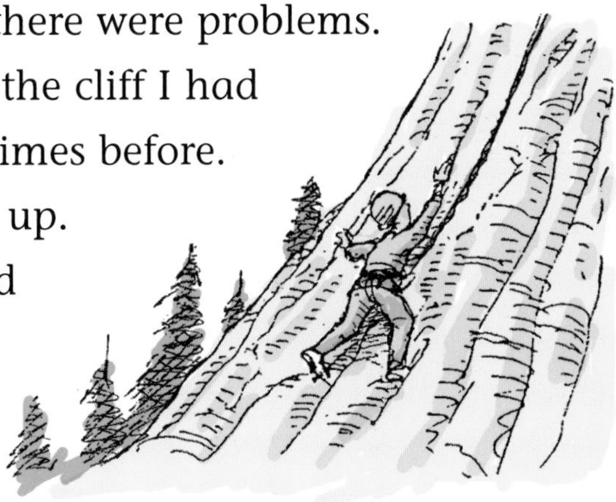

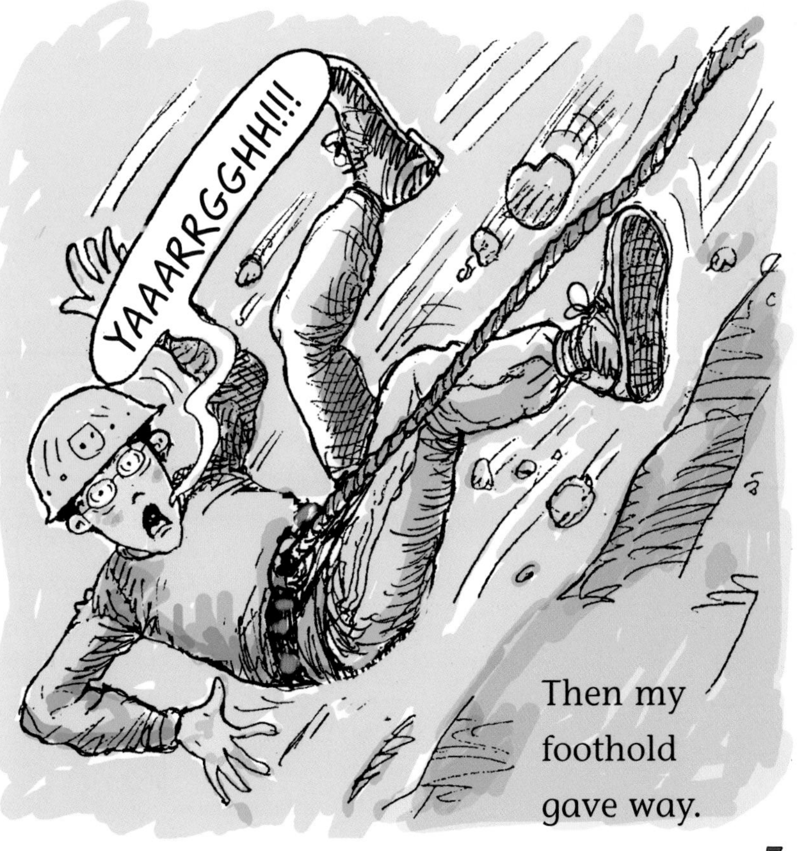
YAAARRGGHH!!!

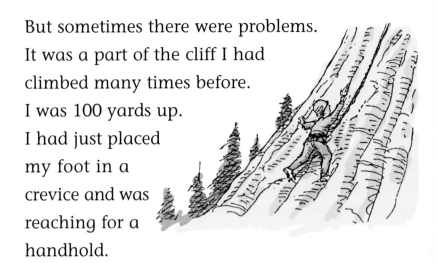

Then my foothold gave way.

Luckily, my safety harness and rope held, but I was really scared.

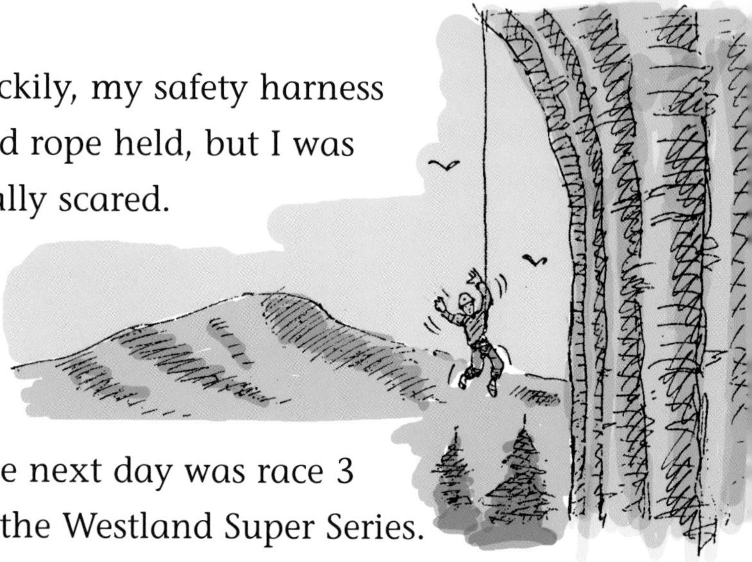

The next day was race 3 of the Westland Super Series. 11 o'clock. First run.
I was waiting at the starting line, with Dozy and Andy behind me. I thought I felt fine.

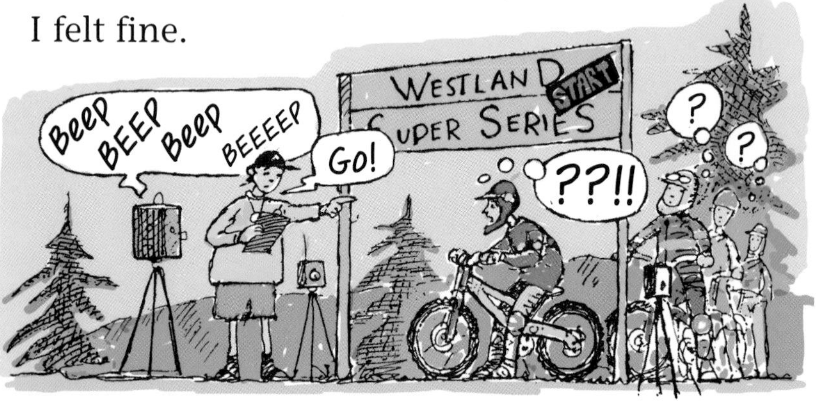
Beep BEEP Beep BEEEEP
Go!
WESTLAND SUPER SERIES
START
??!!
?
?

Suddenly, I couldn't move. I felt like my feet were nailed to the floor!

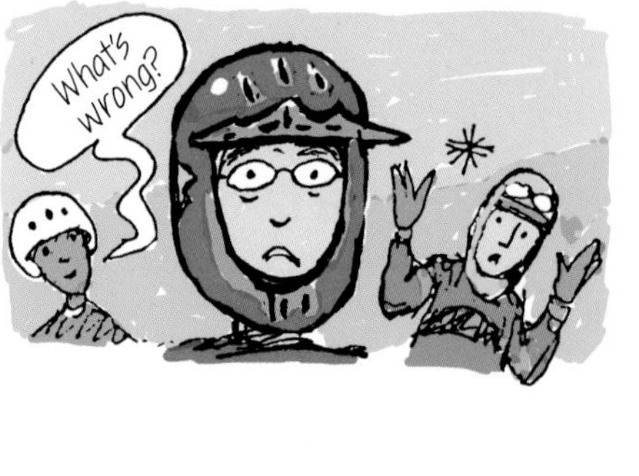
What's wrong?

I was shaking all over, so before the next run, I went back to the food tent for a drink. I felt a little better until I overheard my friends talking.

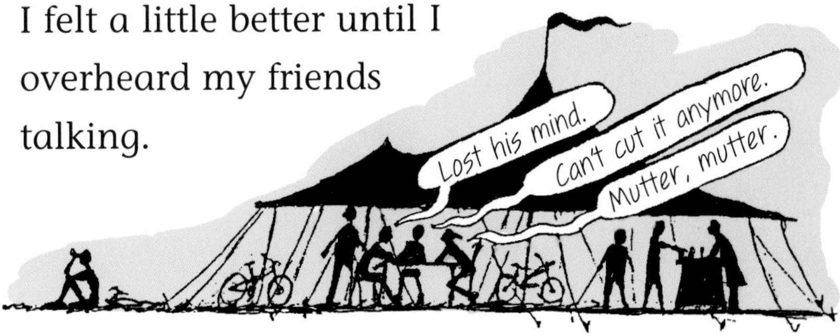
Lost his mind.
Can't cut it anymore.
Mutter, mutter.

In spite of all this, I managed to do okay for my second run. I was really starting to feel much better, until I got to the first dropoff on the course.

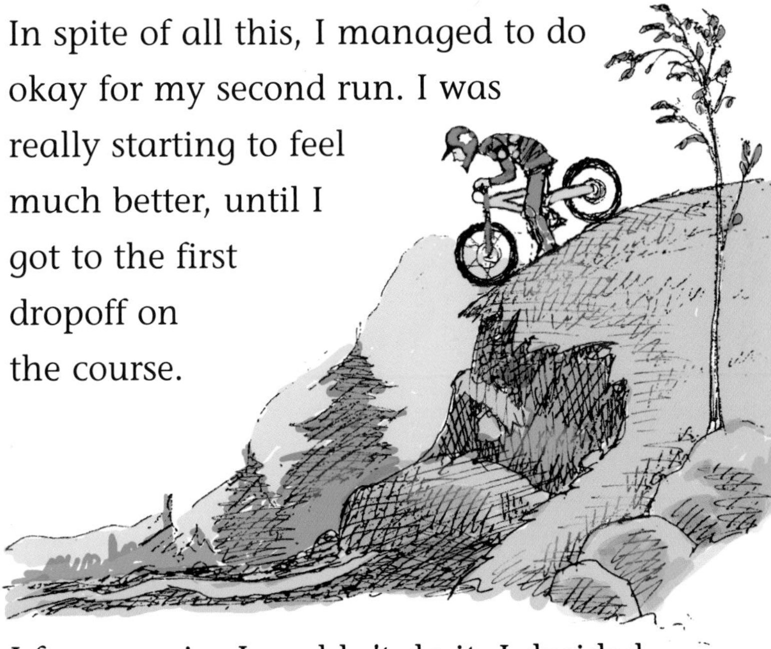

I froze again. I couldn't do it. I decided to walk that one, and the next one, too. I came in 14th. What a disaster!

There was only one thing to do — serious training on the big drops above Westridge Cliff. It was a long, long walk up, but it was the best place to get over my fear of heights.

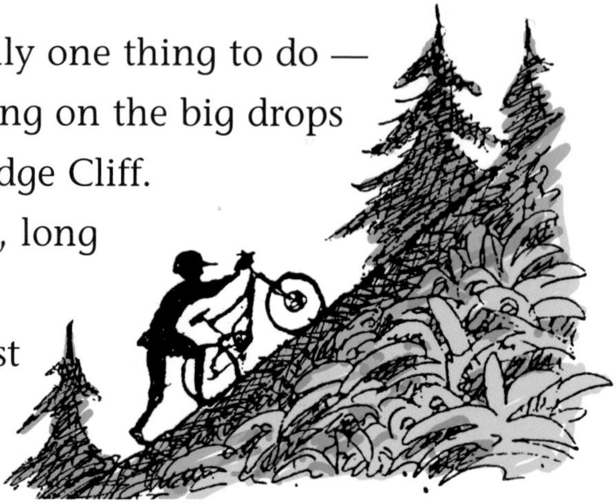

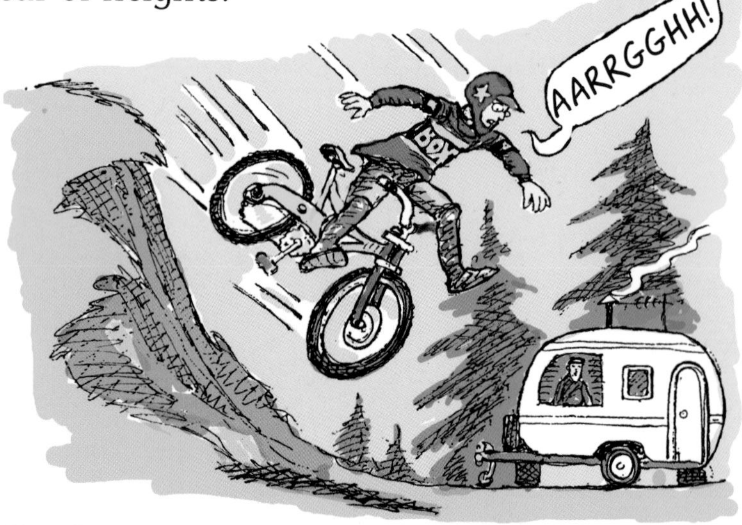

AARRGGHH!

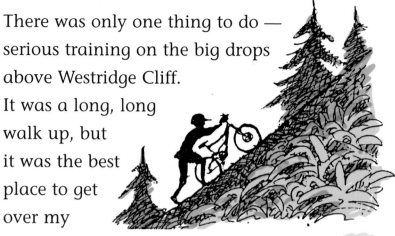

All I did was make myself even more scared.

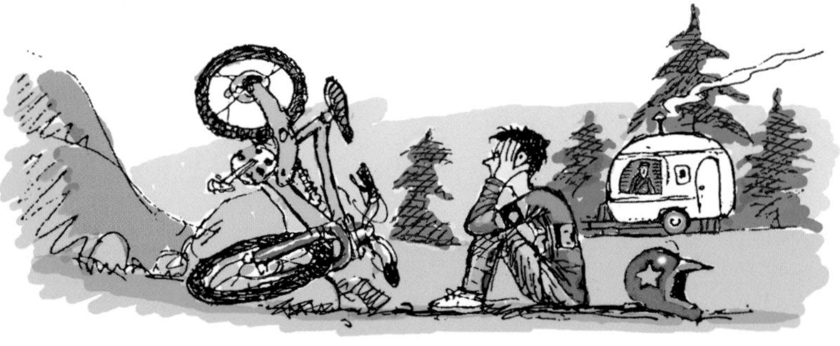

After a really bad crash, old Jack, the forest ranger who lived in a trailer on top of the cliff, walked over and said . . .

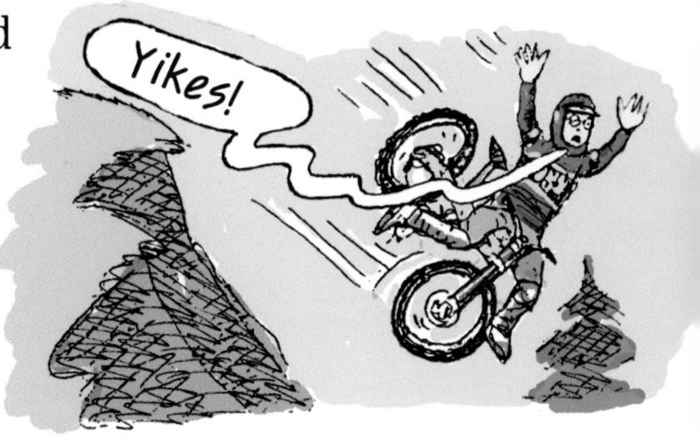
Yikes!

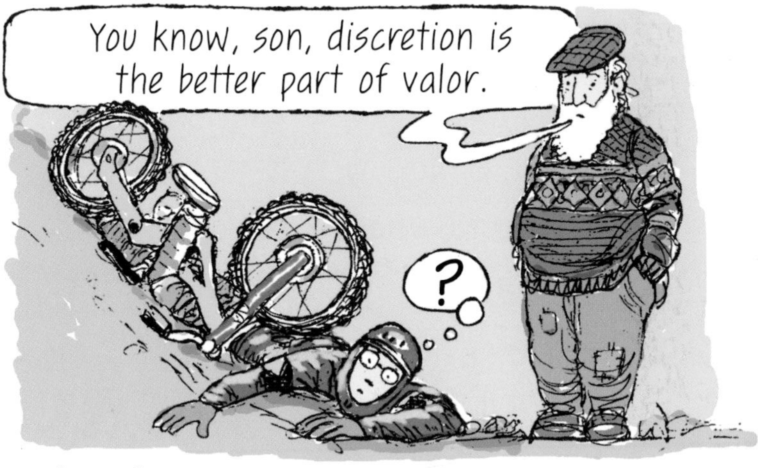
You know, son, discretion is the better part of valor.
?

Later that day . . .

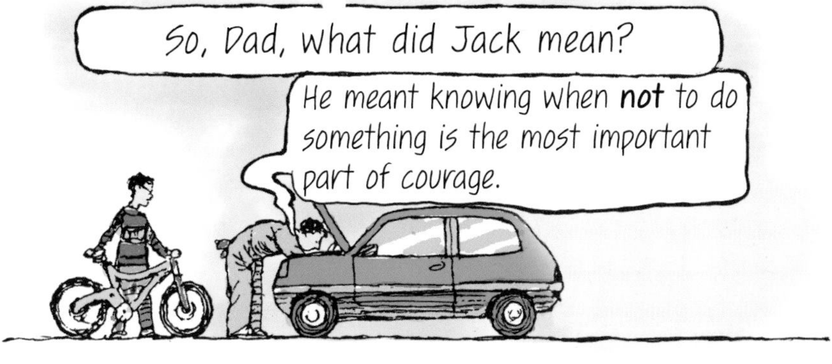
So, Dad, what did Jack mean?
He meant knowing when **not** to do something is the most important part of courage.

Dozy came up to the cliff dropoffs the next day to try to help me with my problems.

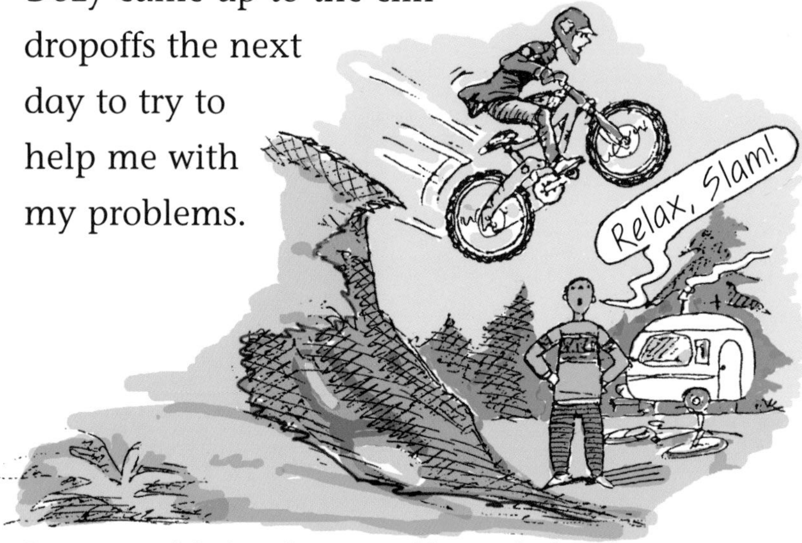
Relax, Slam!

But I couldn't relax at all. And then I bent my front wheel. I was thinking angrily about the long walk back with a useless bike when I heard a crash!

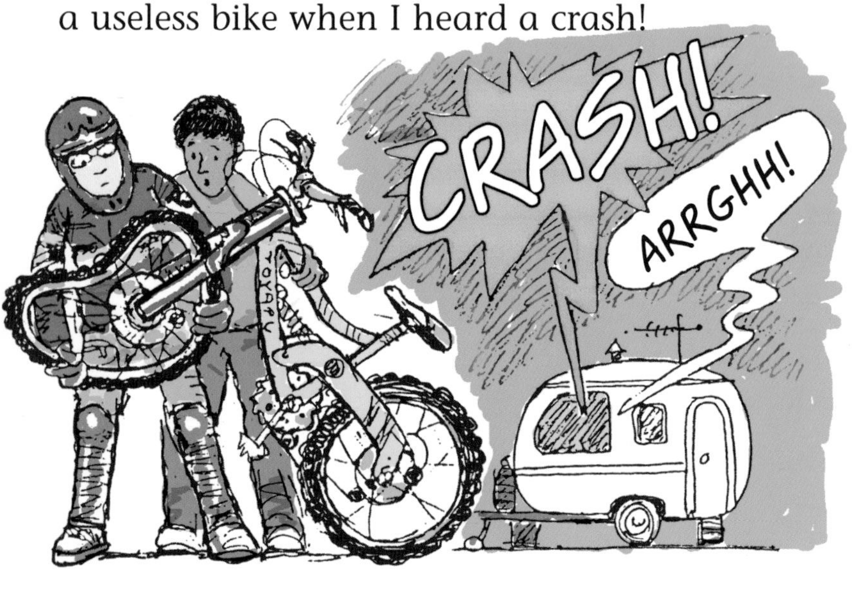
CRASH!
ARRGHH!

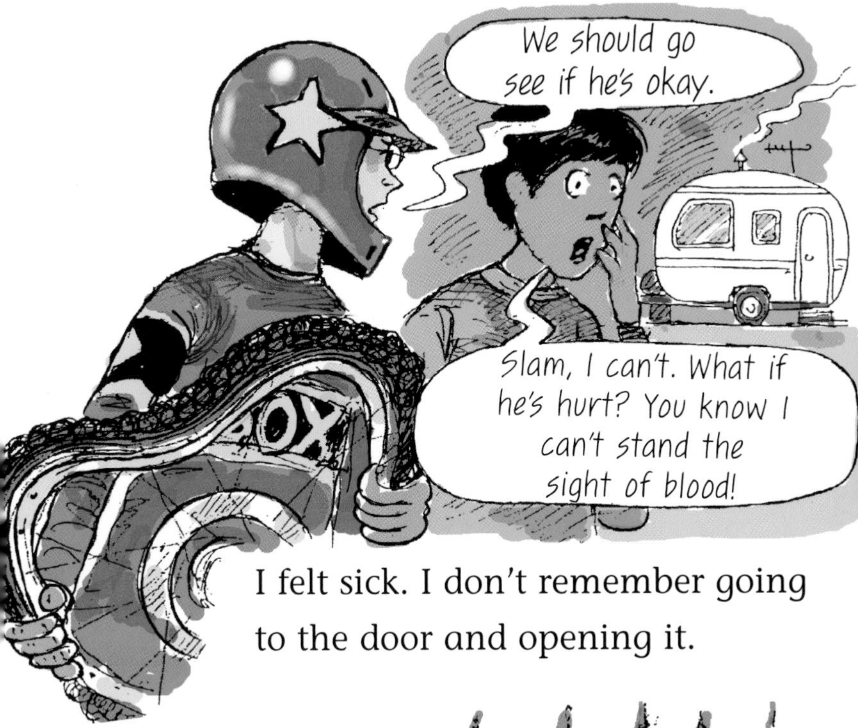
We should go see if he's okay.
Slam, I can't. What if he's hurt? You know I can't stand the sight of blood!

I felt sick. I don't remember going to the door and opening it.

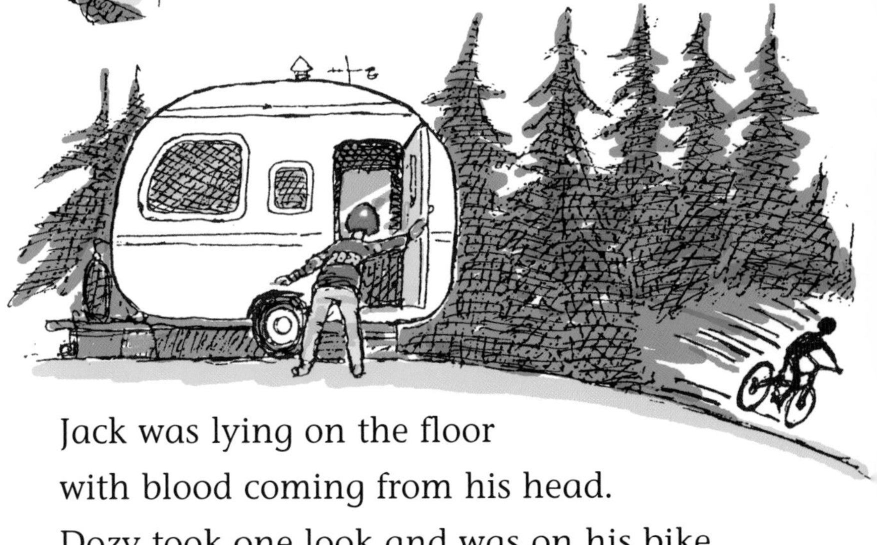

Jack was lying on the floor
with blood coming from his head.
Dozy took one look and was on his bike.

I had to get help up to Jake's trailer (1),
but I was faced with a horrible choice.
I could either climb down Westridge
Cliff (2) without ropes and then
run into the town (3),
which would
take about
20 minutes.

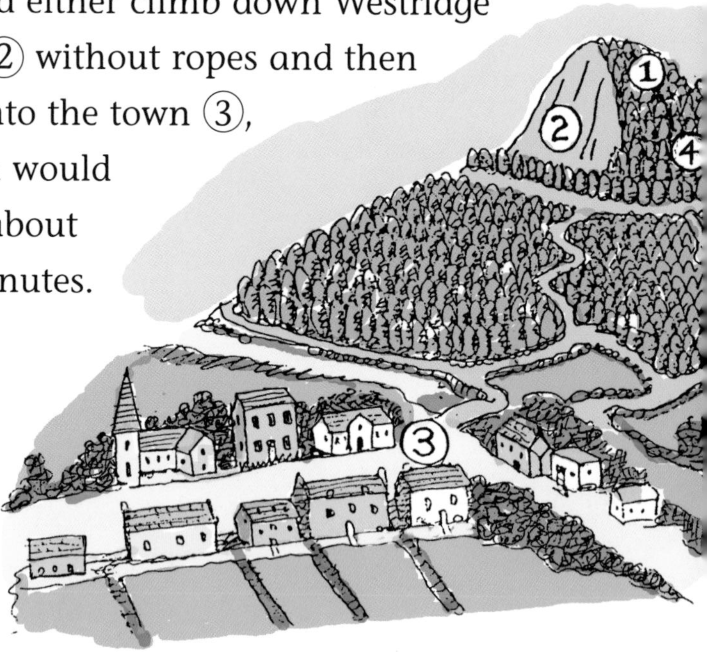
1
2
4
3

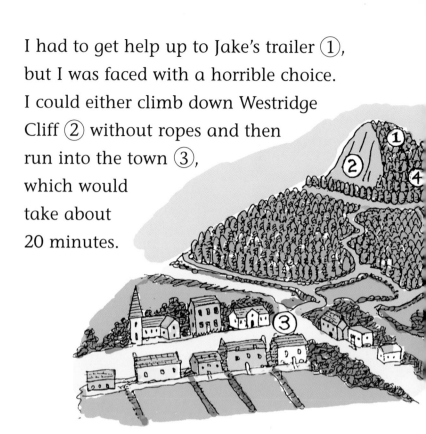

Or I could get back home using the slow trail
through the woods (4), which was easy to
ride but hard to run.
If only I hadn't
broken my
wheel! If only
Dozy hadn't
taken off!

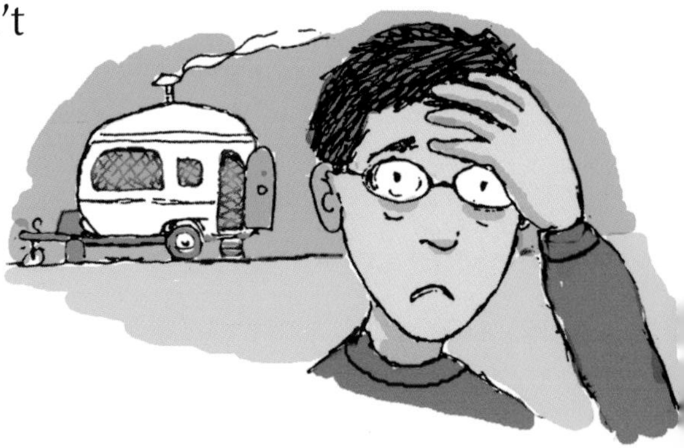

I just couldn't decide what to do. In my mind's eye I saw two newspaper headlines:

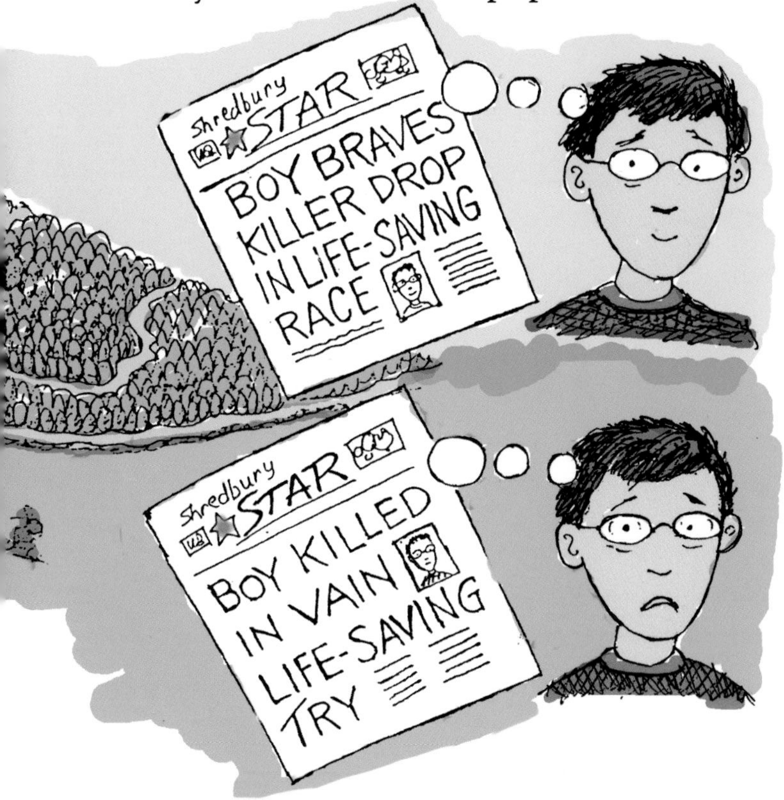
Shredbury STAR
BOY BRAVES KILLER DROP IN LIFE-SAVING RACE
Shredbury STAR
BOY KILLED IN VAIN LIFE-SAVING TRY

Then I remembered Jack's advice.

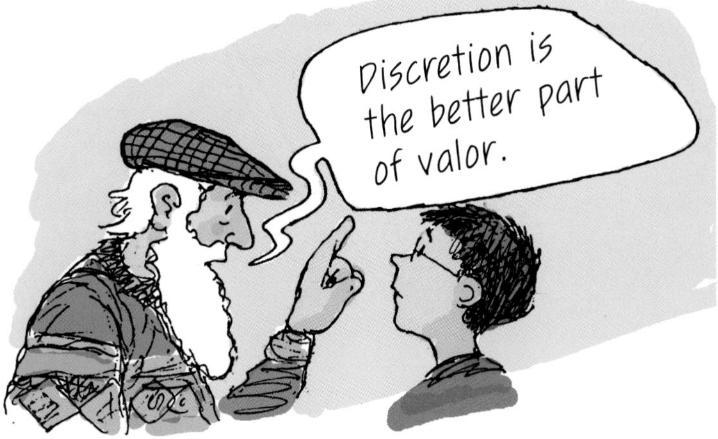
Discretion is the better part of valor.

I ignored it.

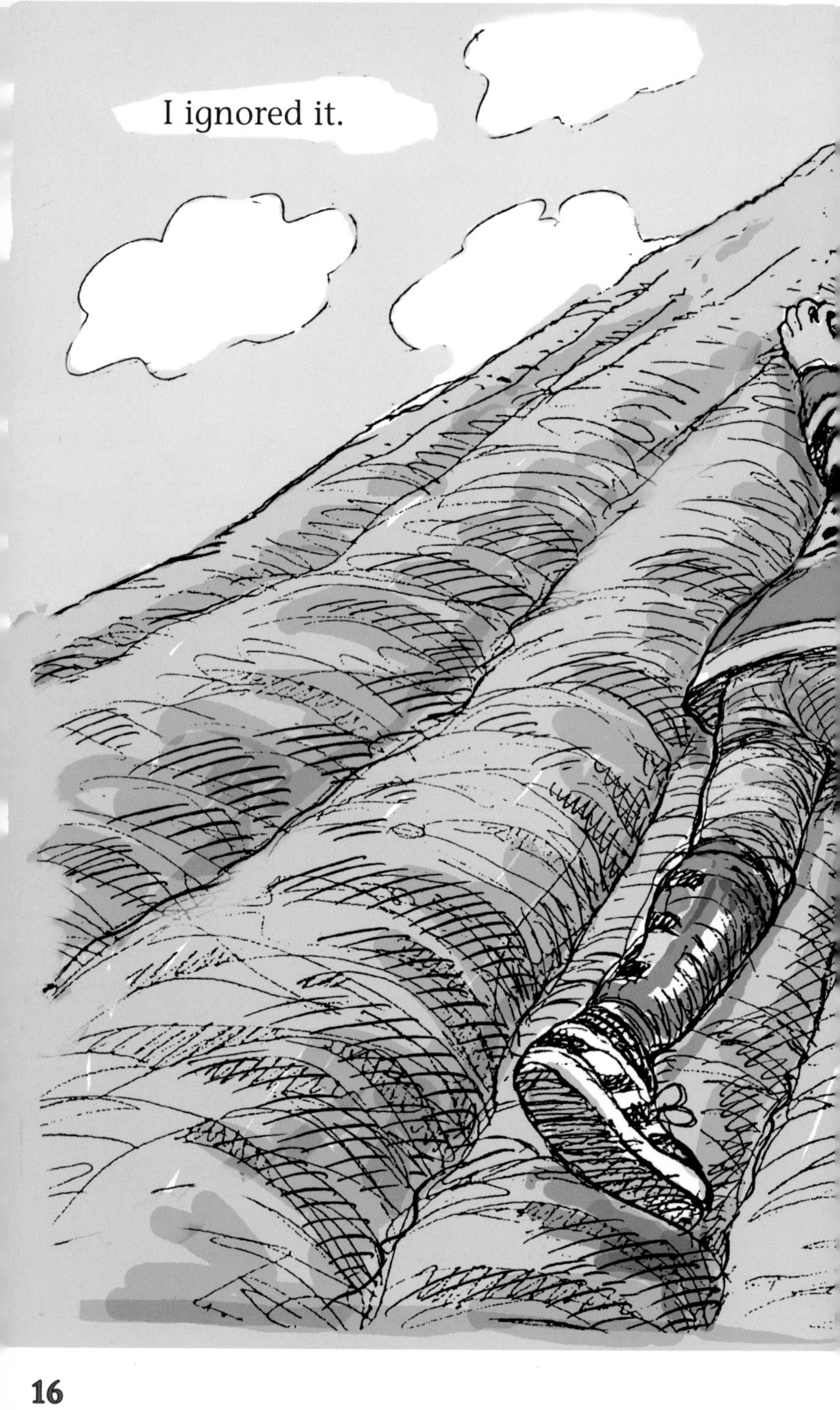

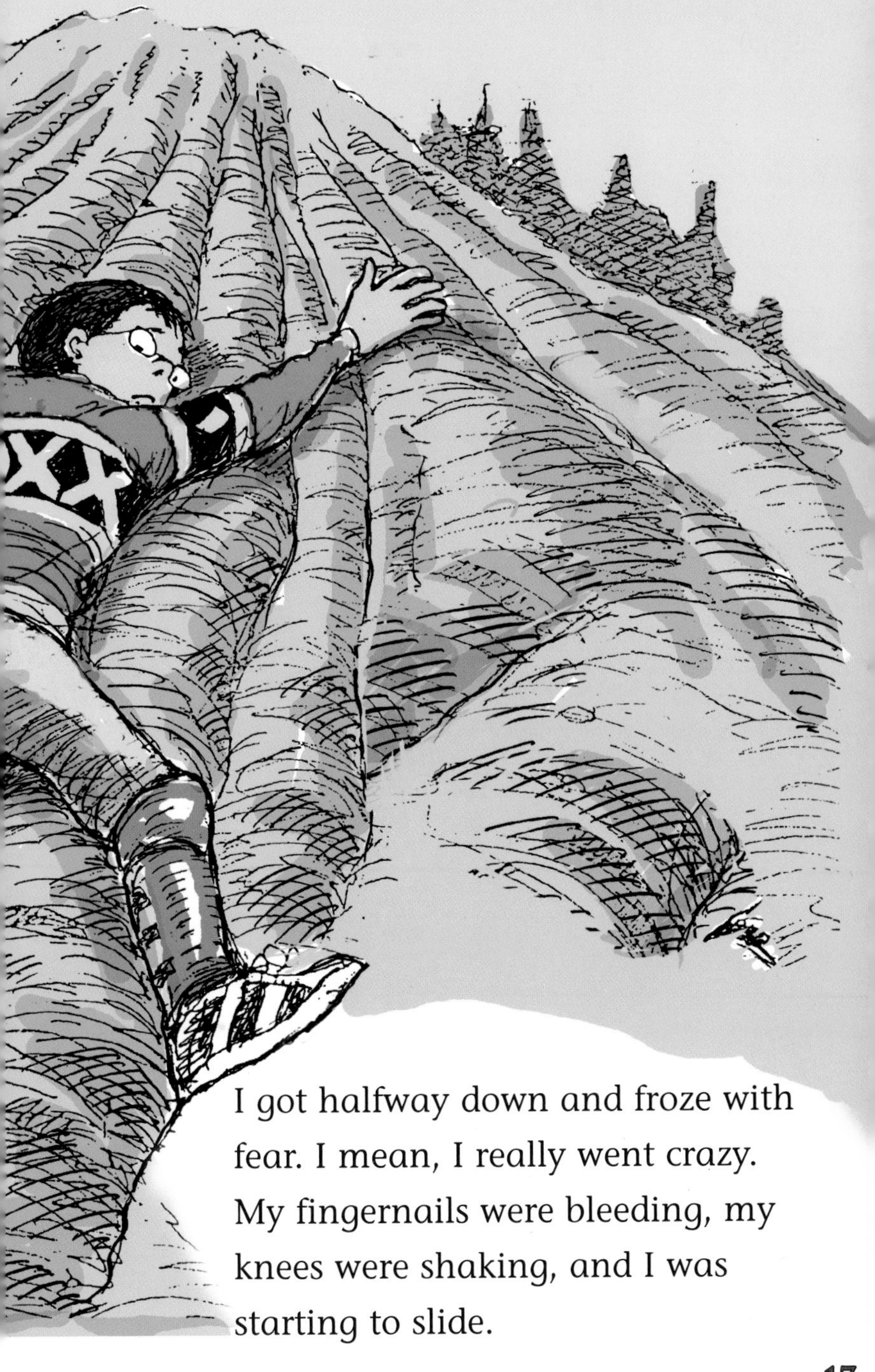

I got halfway down and froze with fear. I mean, I really went crazy. My fingernails were bleeding, my knees were shaking, and I was starting to slide.

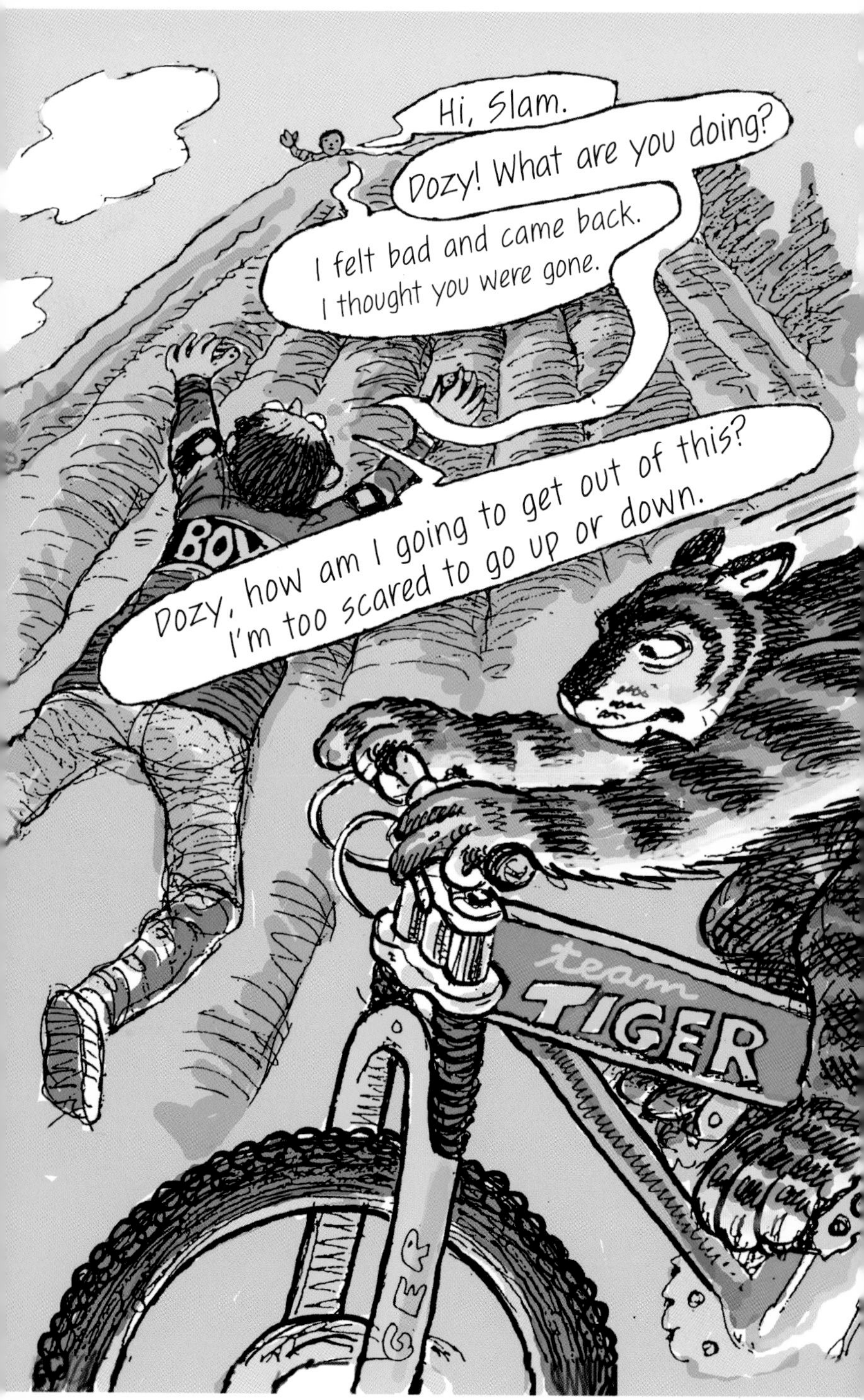
Hi, Slam.
Dozy! What are you doing?
I felt bad and came back. I thought you were gone.
Dozy, how am I going to get out of this? I'm too scared to go up or down.
team TIGER

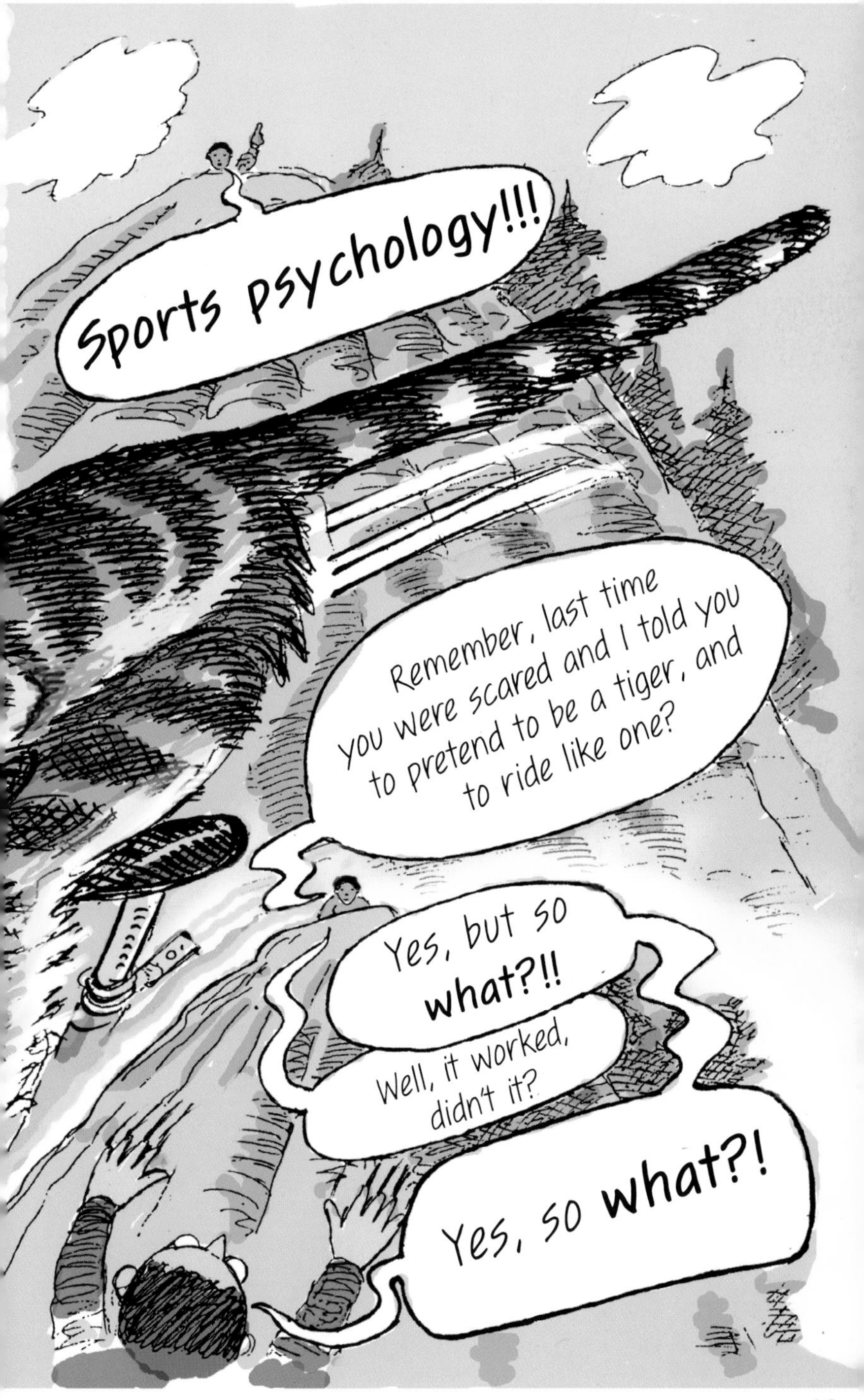
Sports psychology!!!
Remember, last time you were scared and I told you to pretend to be a tiger, and to ride like one?
Yes, but so **what?!!**
Well, it worked, didn't it?
Yes, so **what?!**

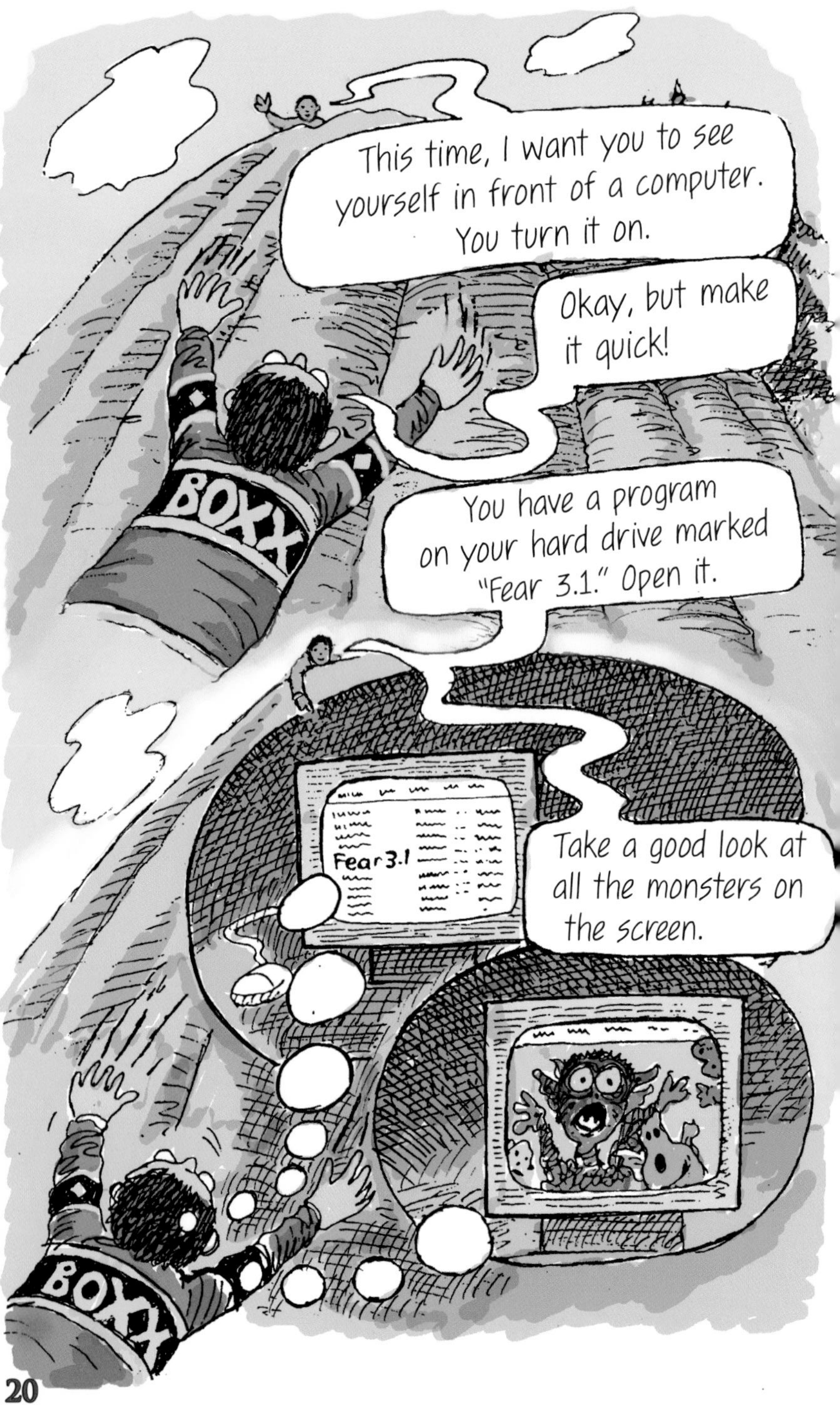
This time, I want you to see yourself in front of a computer. You turn it on.
Okay, but make it quick!
You have a program on your hard drive marked "Fear 3.1." Open it.
Take a good look at all the monsters on the screen.
BOXX
Fear 3.1
BOXX

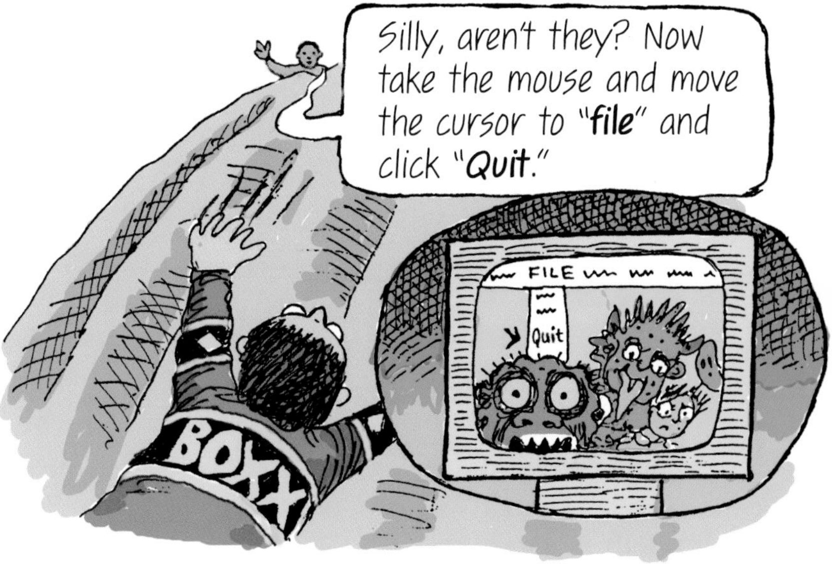
Silly, aren't they? Now take the mouse and move the cursor to "**file**" and click "**Quit**."
FILE
Quit
BOXX

Suddenly I felt better. The program was closed. The monsters were gone. My right foot felt for a toehold. My left hand found a crack. One move at a time, I inched my way to the top.

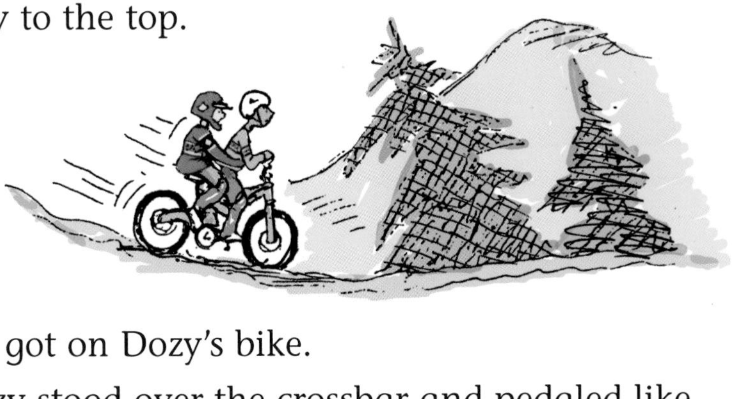

We got on Dozy's bike.
Dozy stood over the crossbar and pedaled like crazy. We were back in town in 20 minutes.

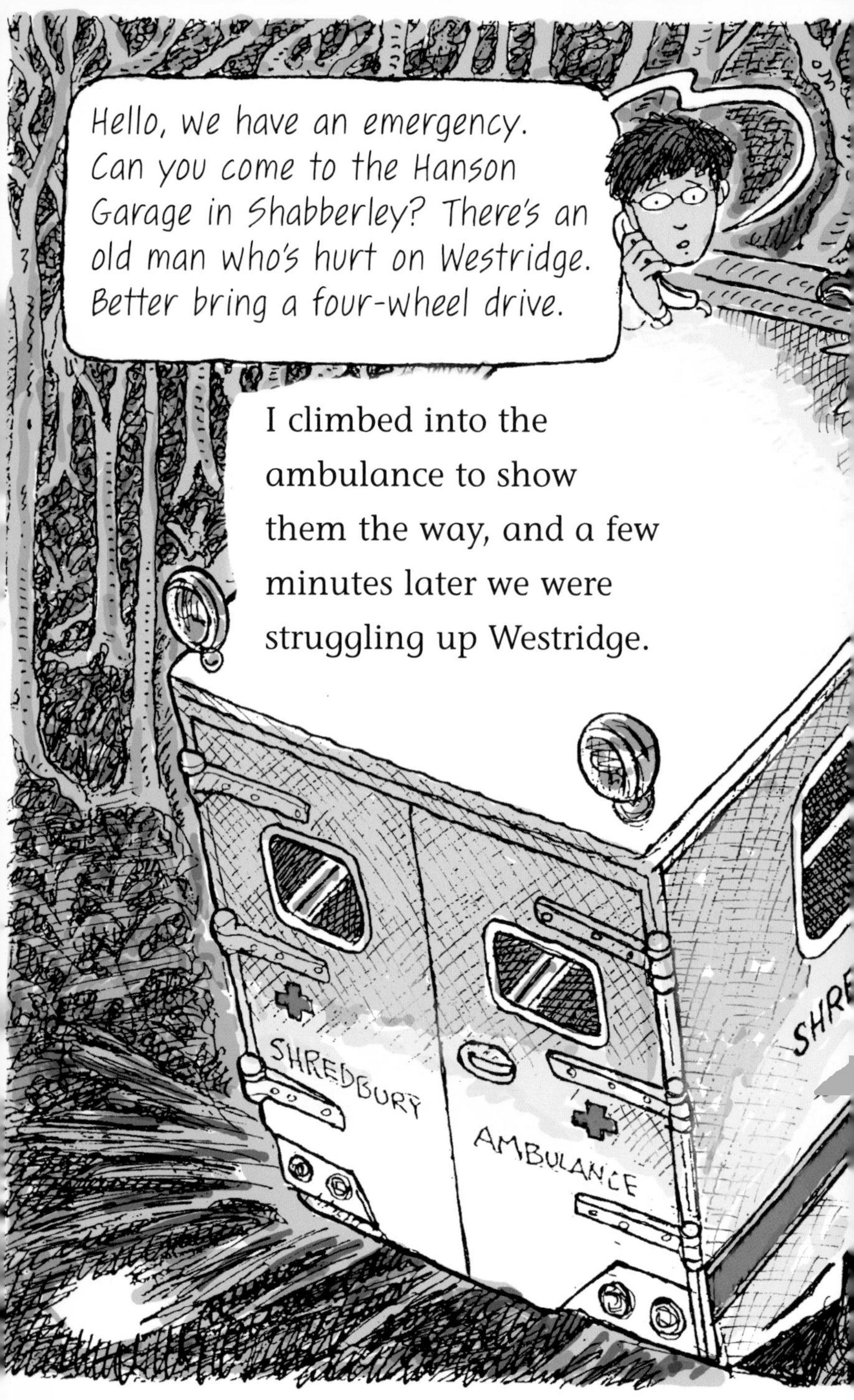
Hello, we have an emergency. Can you come to the Hanson Garage in Shabberley? There's an old man who's hurt on Westridge. Better bring a four-wheel drive.
SHREDBURY
AMBULANCE
SHRE

I climbed into the ambulance to show them the way, and a few minutes later we were struggling up Westridge.

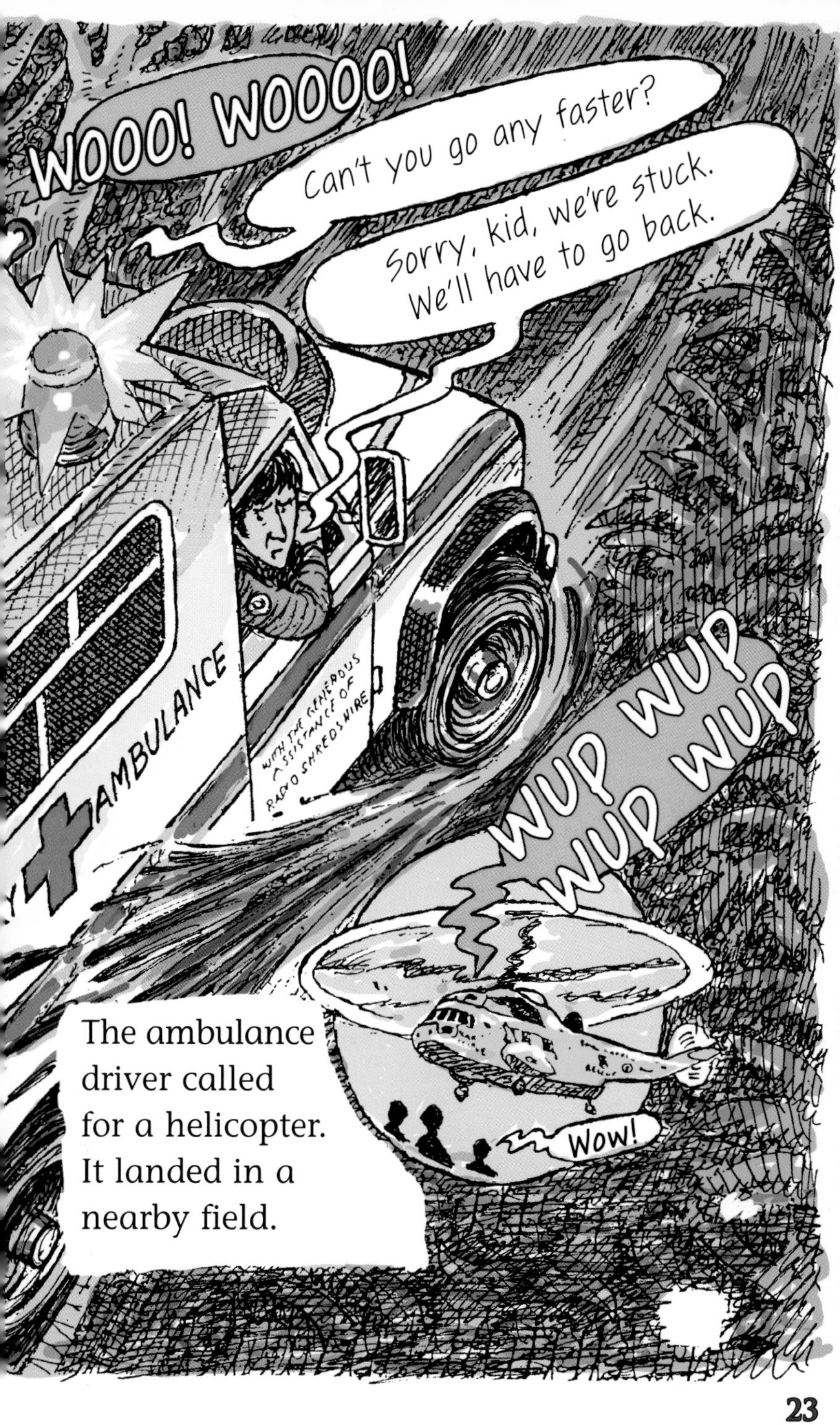
WOOO! WOOOO!
Can't you go any faster?
Sorry, kid, we're stuck. We'll have to go back.
AMBULANCE
WITH THE GENEROUS ASSISTANCE OF RADIO SHREDSHIRE
WUP WUP WUP WUP
Wow!

The ambulance driver called for a helicopter. It landed in a nearby field.

The pilot ran over and asked me to show him Jack's trailer on the map of Westridge.

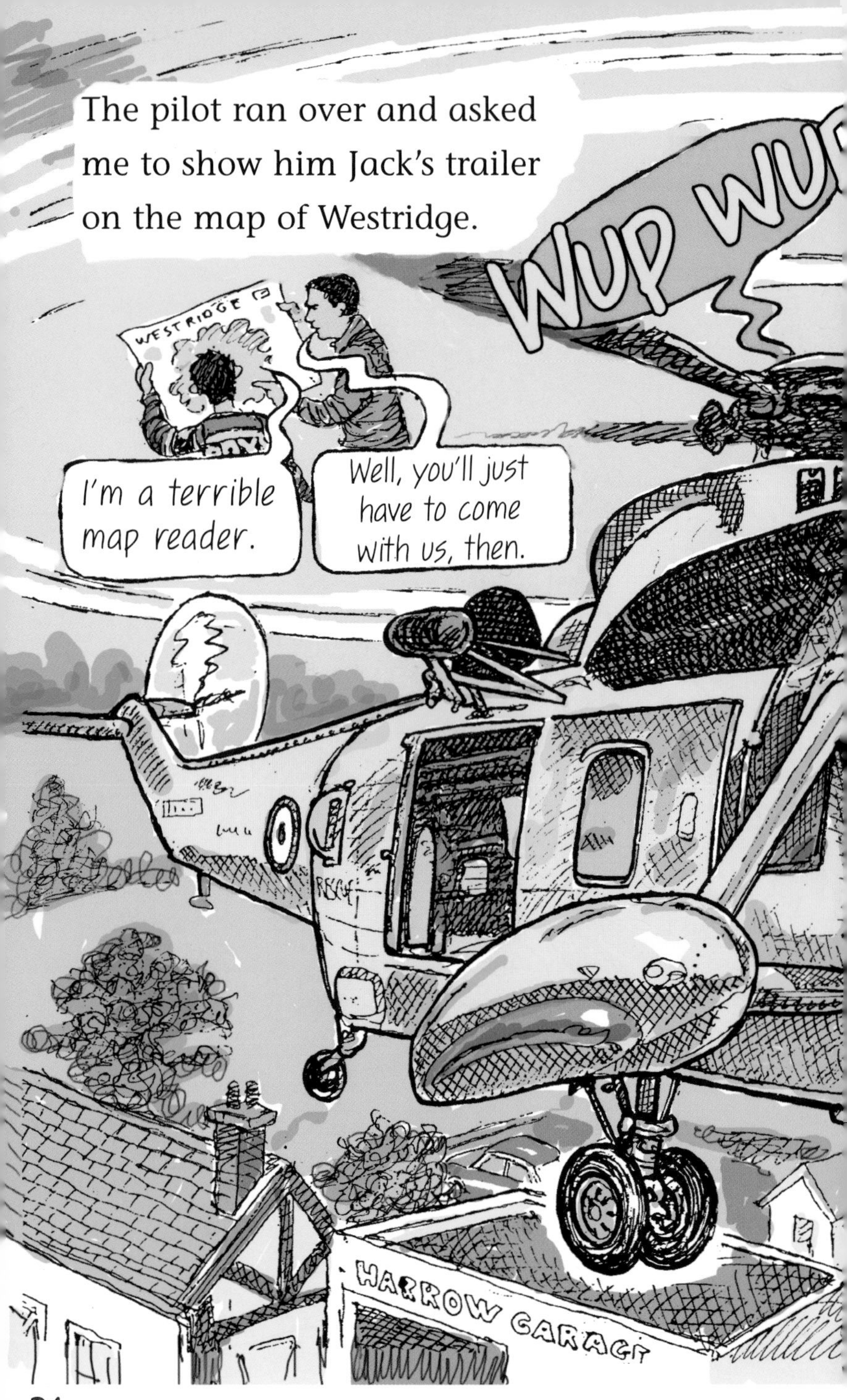
WUP WU
WESTRIDGE
I'm a terrible map reader.
Well, you'll just have to come with us, then.
HARROW GARAGE

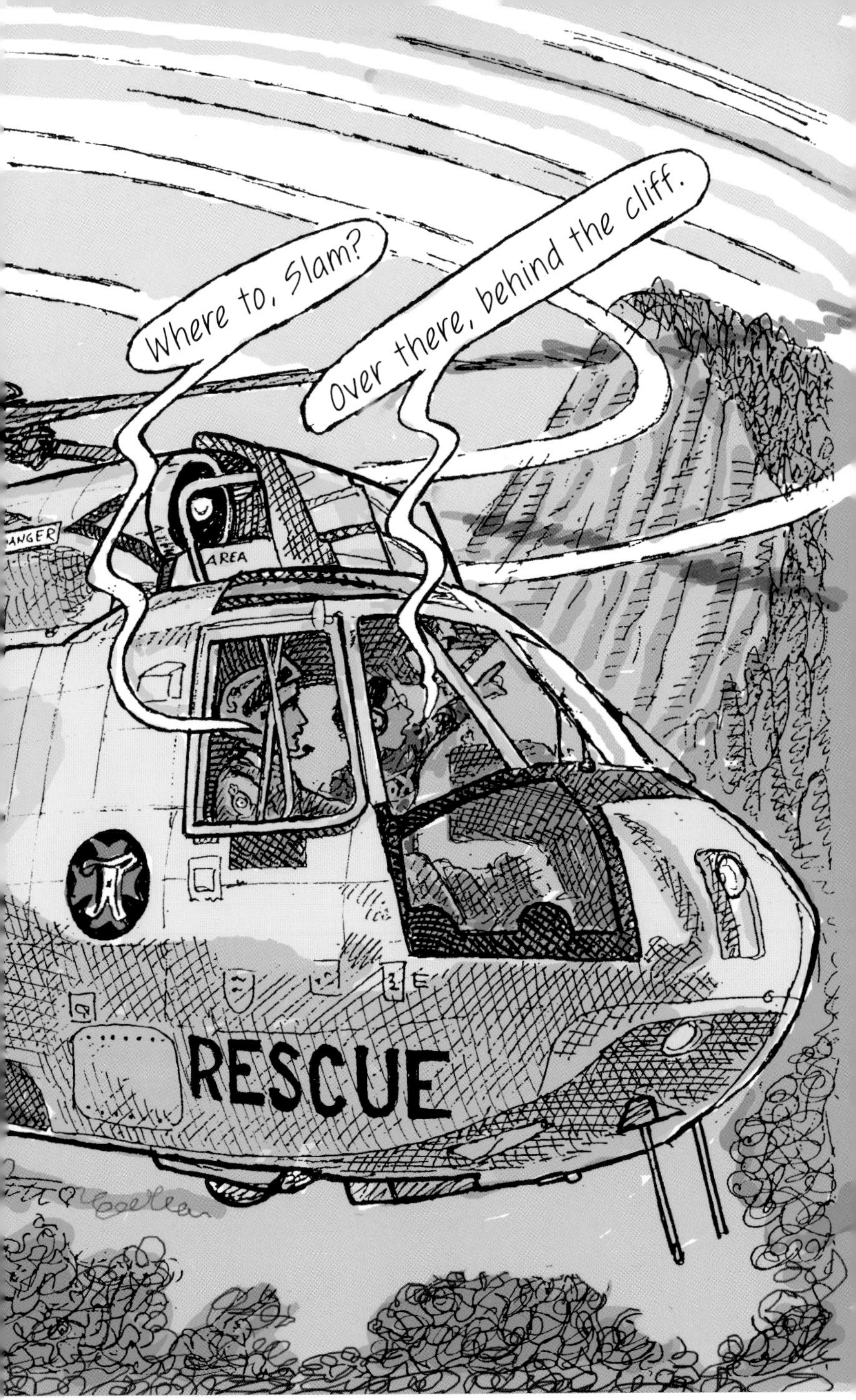
Where to, Slam?
Over there, behind the cliff.
AREA
RESCUE

But when we got there, it didn't make sense.

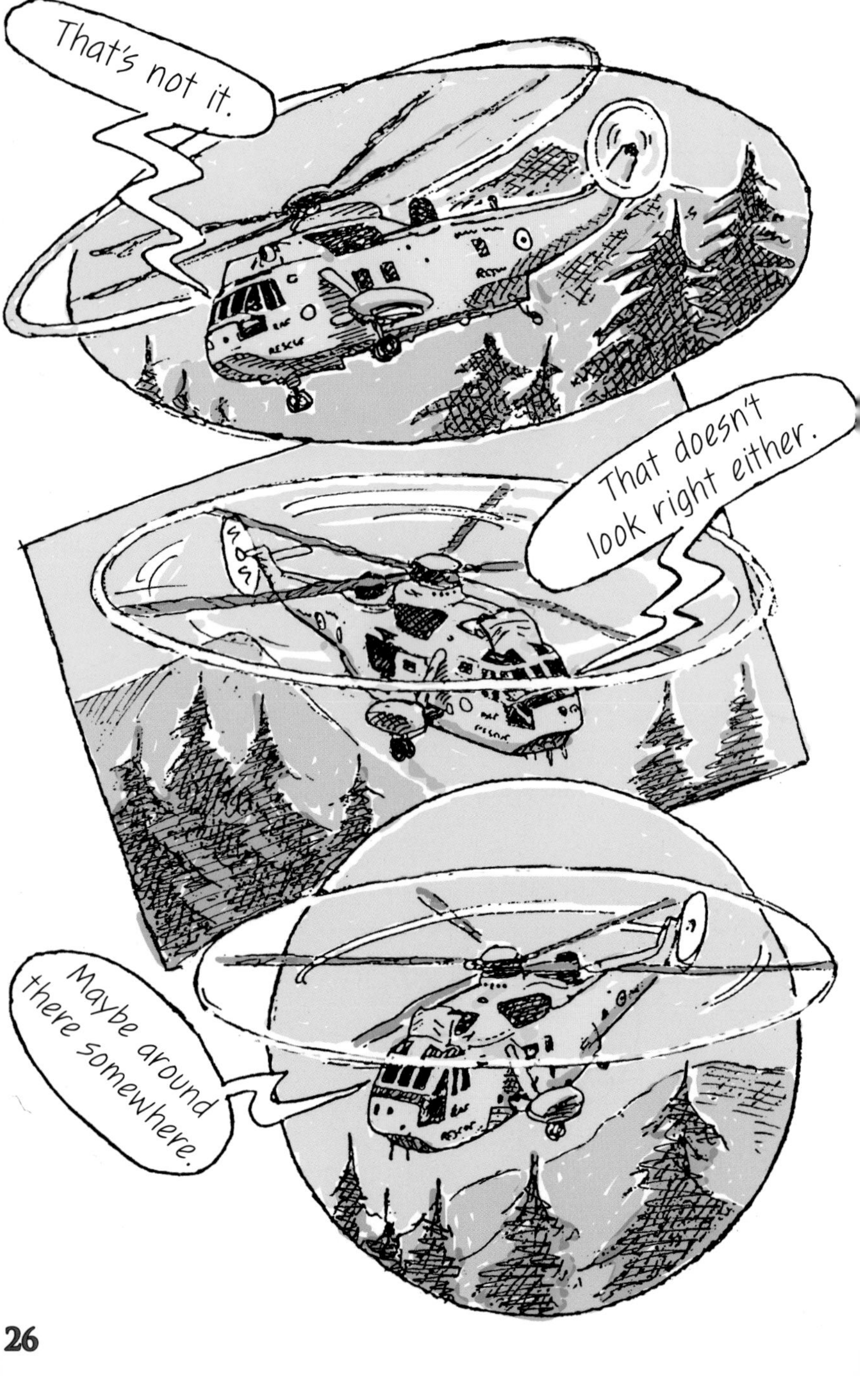
That's not it.
That doesn't look right either.
Maybe around there somewhere.

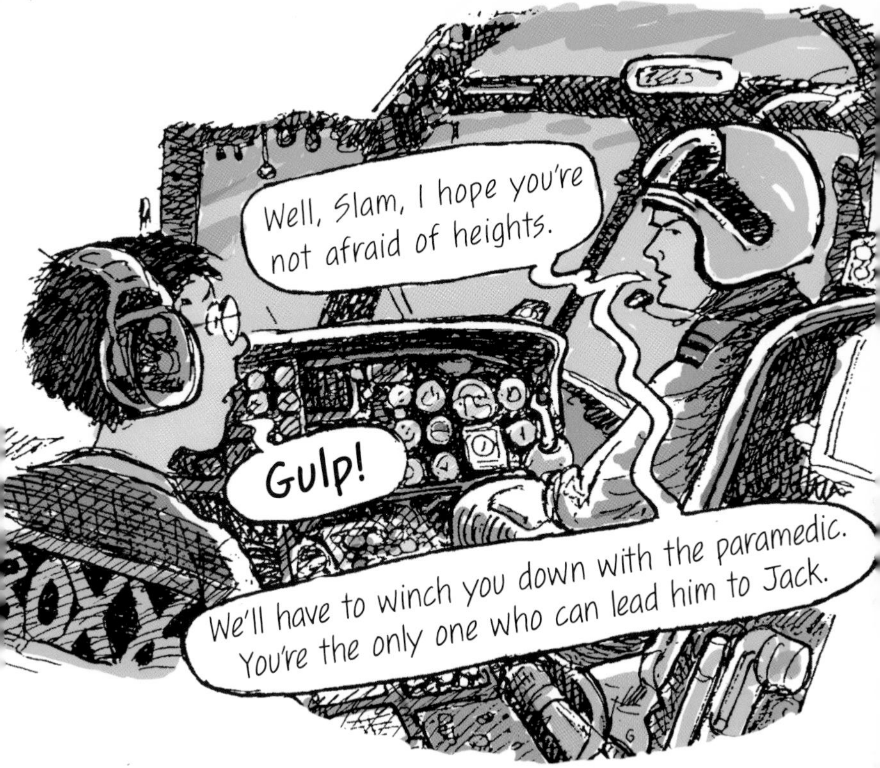
Well, Slam, I hope you're not afraid of heights.
Gulp!
We'll have to winch you down with the paramedic. You're the only one who can lead him to Jack.

And so, there I was, with nothing between me and the trees, 100 yards below.

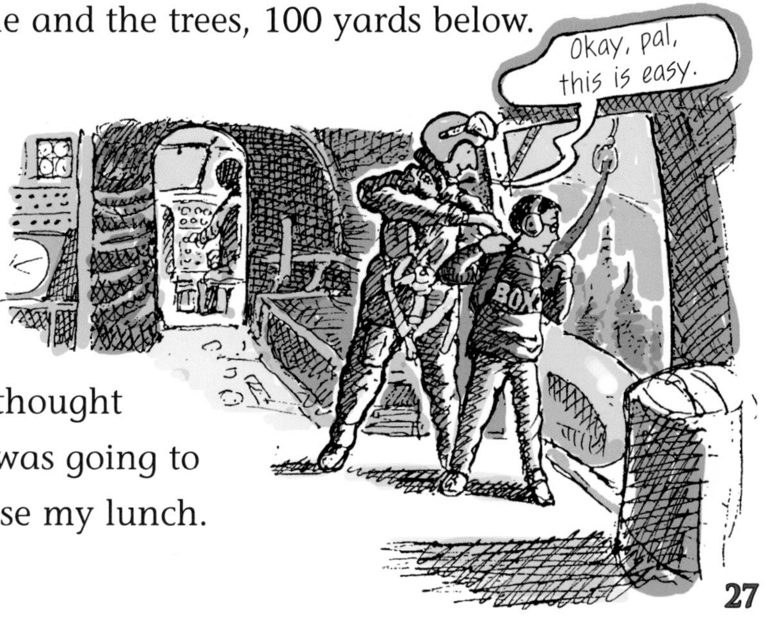
Okay, pal, this is easy.

I thought
I was going to
lose my lunch.

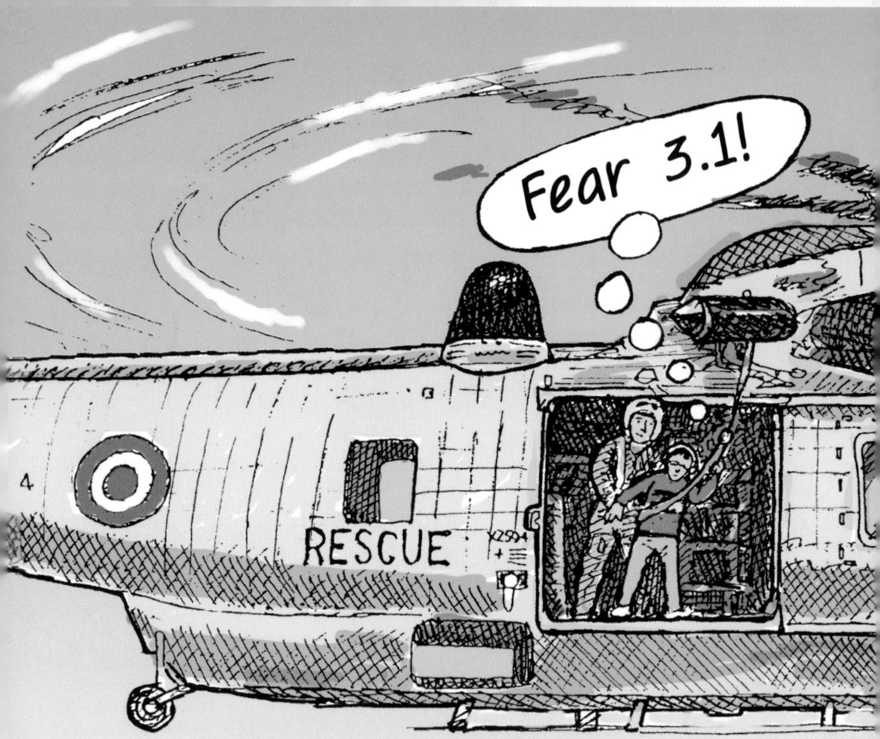

Fear 3.1!
RESCUE

I opened the computer program.
I looked at the monsters.
I moved the cursor to "File."
I clicked "Quit."

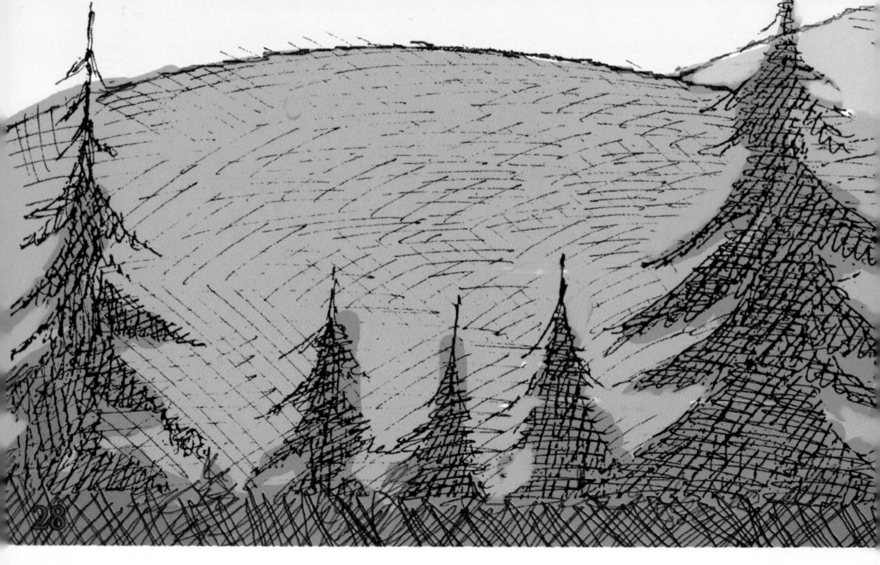

I took a deep breath and jumped out of the door of the helicopter.

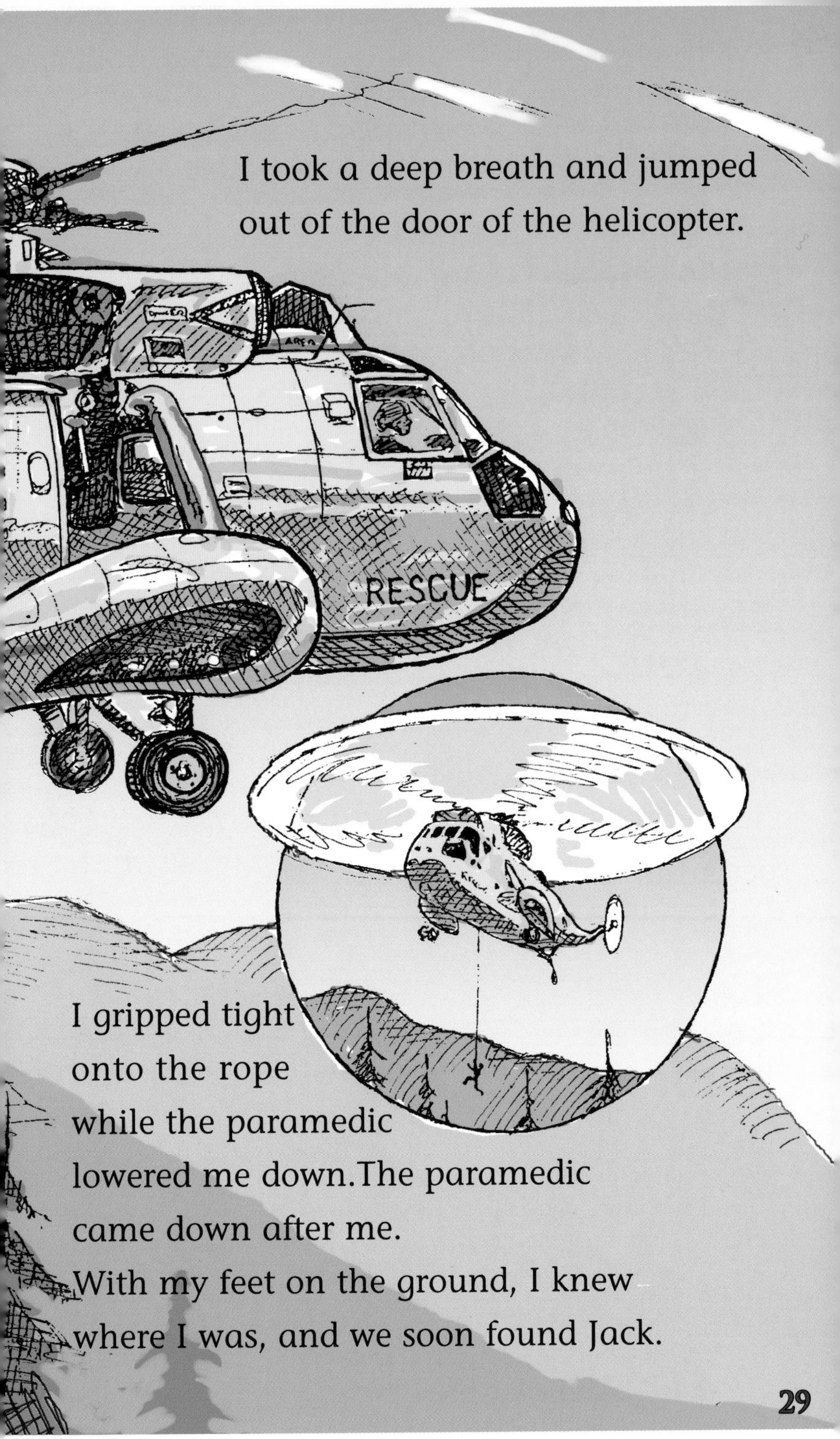
RESCUE

I gripped tight onto the rope while the paramedic lowered me down. The paramedic came down after me.
With my feet on the ground, I knew where I was, and we soon found Jack.

Jack had turned a really funny color, and his breathing was very odd.

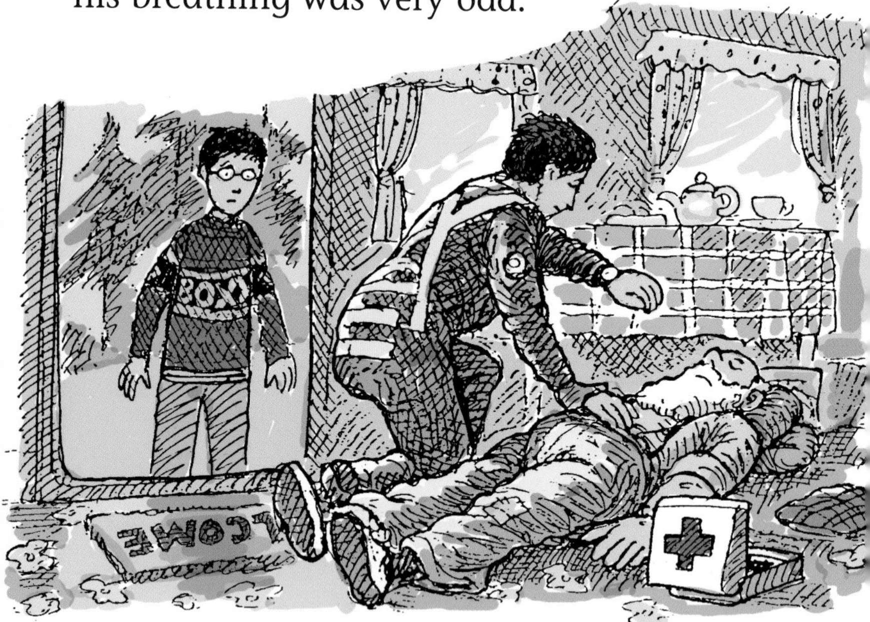

The paramedic radioed our exact position to the helicopter. The pilot hovered over the van, and lowered a special stretcher, called a Stokes litter, to lift Jack out.

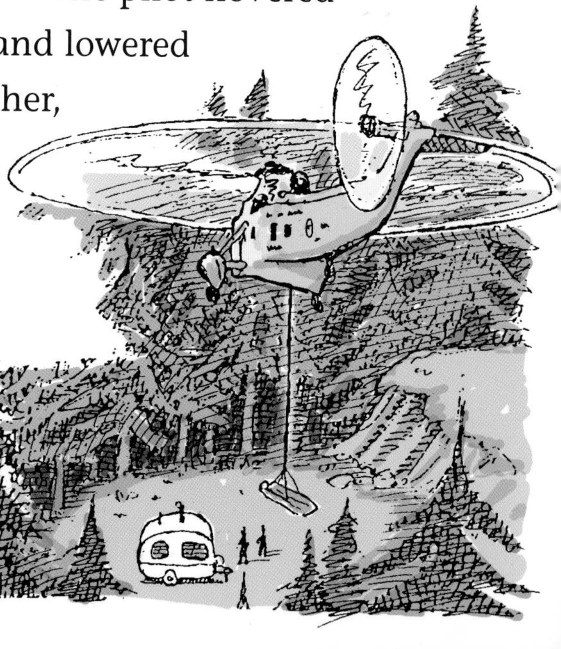

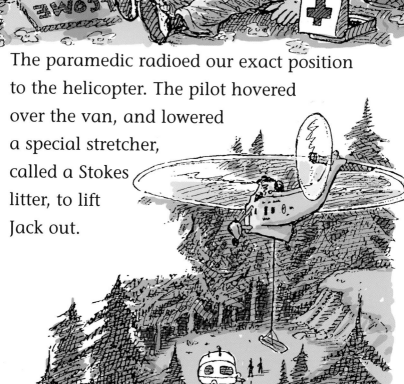

First Jack was lifted up on the stretcher, then me on the rope, then the paramedic.

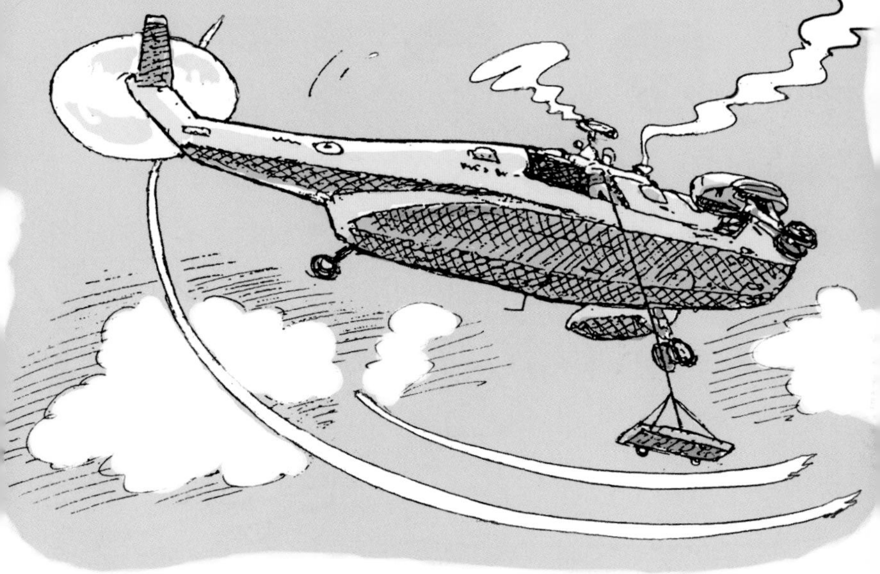

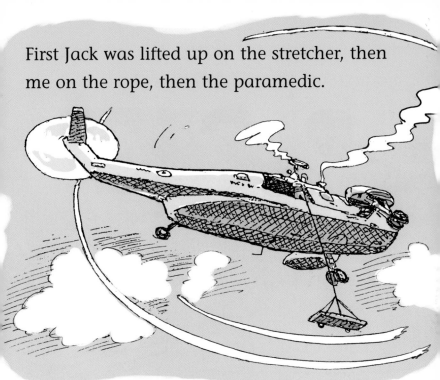

Ten minutes later, we landed on the helipad at Shredbury Hospital. Jack was rushed in on a stretcher.

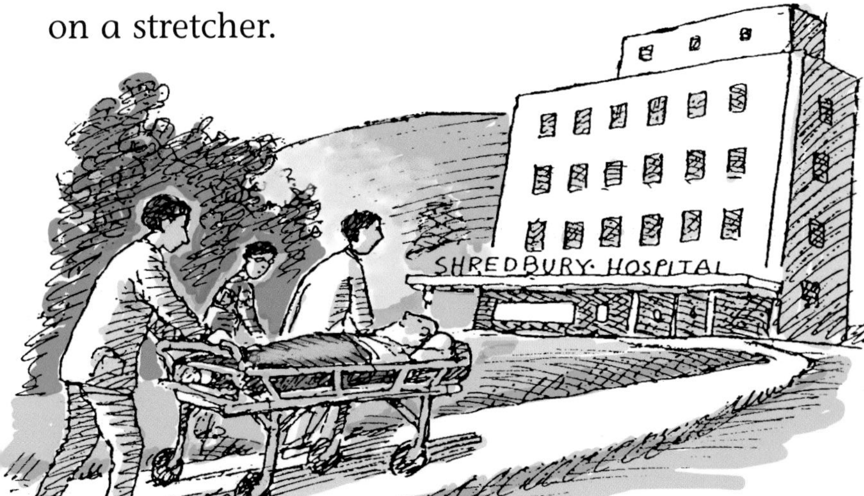
SHREDBURY· HOSPITAL

The next day, we went to see Jack in the hospital. He looked a whole lot better.

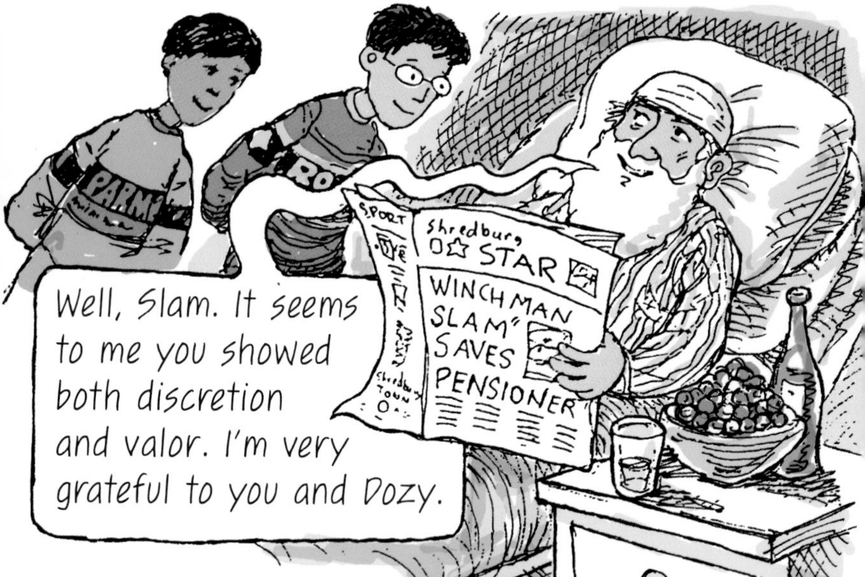
SPORT
Shredbury STAR
WINCHMAN "SLAM" SAVES PENSIONER
Well, Slam. It seems to me you showed both discretion and valor. I'm very grateful to you and Dozy.

But on the way out:

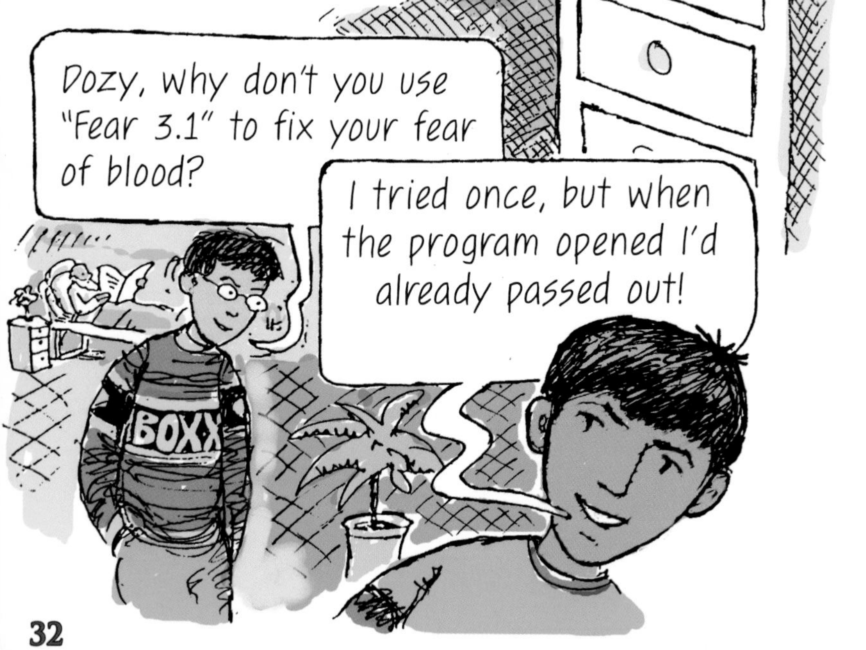
Dozy, why don't you use "Fear 3.1" to fix your fear of blood?
I tried once, but when the program opened I'd already passed out!
BOXX

About the Author and Illustrator

Robin and Chris Lawrie wrote the *Ridge Riders* books together, and Robin illustrated them. Their inspiration for these books is their son. They wanted to write books that he would find interesting. Many of the *Ridge Riders* books are based on adventures he and his friends had while biking.

Robin and Chris live in England, and will soon be moving to a big, old house that is also home to sixty bats.

Glossary

crevice (KREH-viss)—a crack or split in a rock

crossbar (KRAWSS-bahr)—on a bike, the metal bar that runs between the wheels

cursor (KUR-sur)—the arrow or line that shows your position on a computer screen

deaf (DEF)—not able to hear well or hear at all

discretion (diss-CRESH-uhn)—the ability to decide

harness (HAR-niss)—a set of straps that keeps someone safe

paramedic (pa-ruh-MEH-dik)—a person who is trained to do emergency medical work

psychology (sye-KOH-luh-jee)—the study of human behavior, the mind, and emotions

radioed (RAY-dee-ohd)—sent message by radio

valor (VAL-ur)—bravery

Internet Sites

Do you want to know more about subjects related to this book? Or are you interested in learning about other topics? Then check out FactHound, a fun, easy way to find Internet sites.

Our investigative staff has already sniffed out great sites for you!

Here's how to use FactHound:

1. Visit *www.facthound.com*

2. Select your grade level.

3. To learn more about subjects related to this book, type in the book's ISBN number: **1598893483**.

4. Click the **Fetch It** button.

FactHound will fetch the best Internet sites for you!

Discussion Questions

1. What does Jack mean on page 11 when he says "Discretion is the better part of valor"? Do you agree with him or not? What are some ways that you can use discretion to be brave?

2. Are you afraid of anything? How can someone get over their fears? What do you think of "Fear 3.1," the imaginary computer program Dozy invents for Slam?

3. Slam belongs to a scout troop, and it's with that group that he learns about rock climbing. Are you in any groups or teams? What do you learn from them?

Writing Prompts

1. Everyone has fears. What are some of yours? Write a story in which you overcome your greatest fear. If you can't think of one of your own fears, make one up!

2. Slam is forced to face his biggest fear so that he can help save Jack. What would have happened if he had been too scared to go up in the helicopter?

Read other adventures of the Ridge Riders

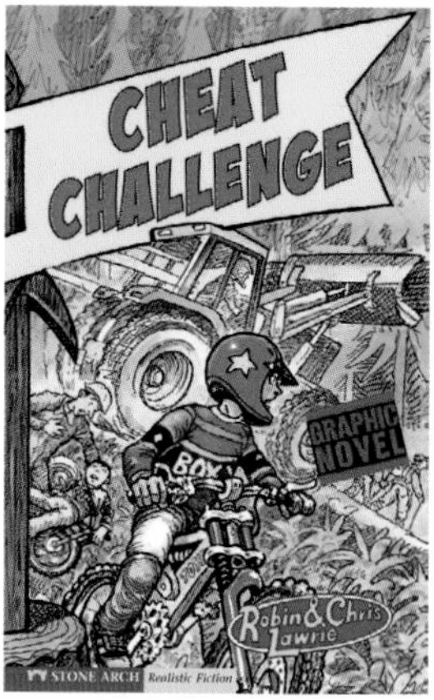
CHEAT CHALLENGE
GRAPHIC NOVEL
Robin & Chris Lawrie
STONE ARCH
Realistic Fiction

Cheat Challenge

Slam Duncan and his friends, the Ridge Riders, don't know what to think when they come across a sword buried deep in their mountain-biking course. It's part of a new racing course contest called Excalibur. Then Slam accidentally gets a look at the map of the course, but he knows he can't tell his teammates the map's secrets.

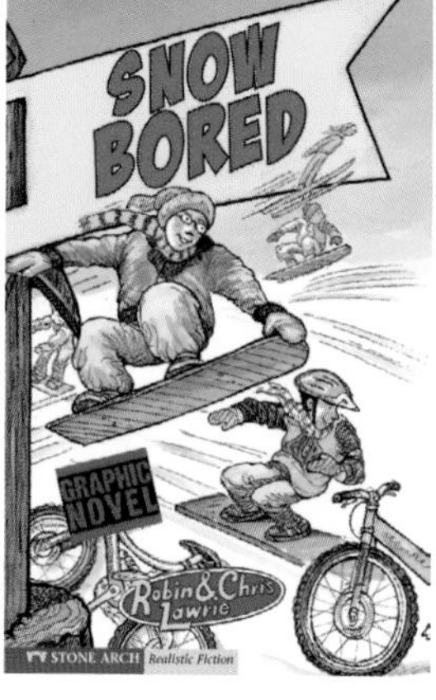
SNOW BORED
GRAPHIC NOVEL
Robin & Chris Lawrie
STONE ARCH
Realistic Fiction

Snow Bored

The Ridge Riders are bored. So much snow has fallen on their mountain biking practice hill that they can't ride. Luckily, Dozy has a great idea. He turns an old skateboard and a pair of sneakers into a snowboard. Before long, everyone is snowboarding.

RADAR RIDERS
GRAPHIC NOVEL
Robin & Chris Lawrie
STONE ARCH Realistic Fiction

Radar Riders

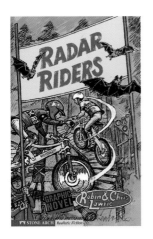

The Ridge Riders need a new place to race, so they build a wild new course. It takes all their skills, and some techno-wizardry, to keep them on track before they run into some unexpected twists and turns.

WHITE LIGHTNING
GRAPHIC NOVEL
Robin & Chris Lawrie
STONE ARCH Realistic Fiction

White Lightning

Someone smashed the Ridge Riders' practice jumps, and they suspect Fiona and her horse-riding friends. The boys are so mean to Fiona that she leaves. Then Slam gets a flat tire and has to race back home to get his spare, and he only has 50 minutes! Now a horse would come in handy!

Check out Stone Arch Books adventure novels!

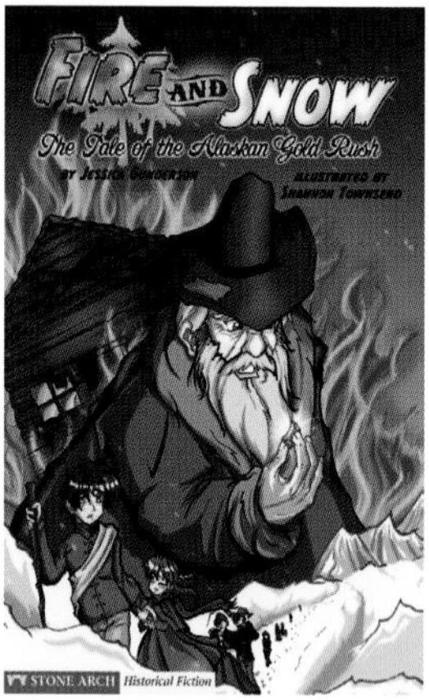
FIRE AND SNOW
The Tale of the Alaskan Gold Rush
STONE ARCH Historical Fiction

Fire and Snow
A Tale of the Alaskan Gold Rush

Ethan and his family leave their comfortable home in Seattle to seek their fortune in the snowy North. Ethan must brave an avalanche, cross an icy river, and battle a deadly fire before he can decide if the hunt for gold is worth the risk.

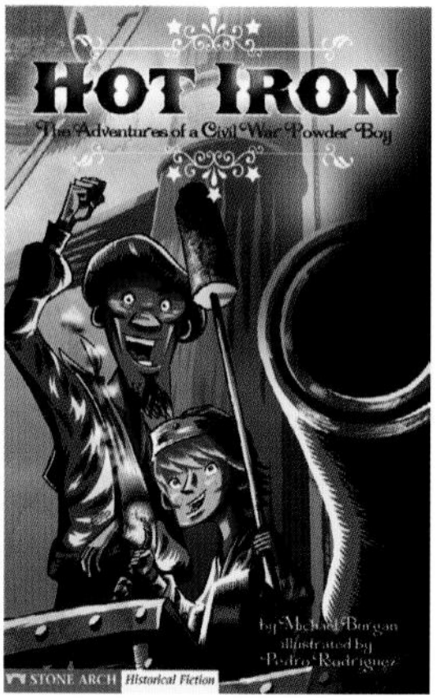
HOT IRON
The Adventures of a Civil War Powder Boy
STONE ARCH Historical Fiction

Hot Iron
The Adventures of a Civil War Powder Boy

Twelve-year-old Charlie O'Leary signs aboard the USS Varuna as it steams its way toward the mouth of the Mississippi River to fight the Confederate Navy. Will his ship survive the awesome Battle of New Orleans?